outpost zero ™

CREATED BY **SEAN KELLEY MCKEEVER** & **ALEXANDRE TEFENKGI**

FOR SKYBOUND ENTERTAINMENT ROBERT KIRKMAN Chairman DAVID
ALPERT CEO SEAN MACKIEWICZ SVP, Editor-in-Chief SHAWN KIRKHAM
SVP, Business Development BRIAN HUNTINGTON VP, Online Content
SHAUNA WYNNE Publicity Director ANDRES JUAREZ Art Director
JON MOISAN Editor ARIELLE BASICH Associate Editor KATE CAUDILL Assistant Editor CARINA TAYLOR
Production Artist PAUL SHIN Business Development Manager JOHNNY O'DELL Social Media Manager
SALLY JACKA Skybound Retailer Relations DAN PETERSEN Sr. Director of Operations & Events Foreign
Rights Inquiries ag@sequentialrights.com Other Licensing Inquiries contact@skybound.com
WWW.SKYBOUND.COM

IMAGE COMICS, INC. ROBERT KIRKMAN Chief Operating Officer ERIK
LARSEN Chief Financial Officer TODD MCFARLANE President MARC
SILVESTRI Chief Executive Officer JIM VALENTINO Vice President ERIC
STEPHENSON Publisher / Chief Creative Officer COREY HART Director of
Sales JEFF BOISON Director of Publishing Planning & Book Trade Sales
CHRIS ROSS Director of Digital Sales JEFF STANG Director of Specialty
Sales KAT SALAZAR Director of PR & Marketing DREW GILL Art Director
HEATHER DOORNINK Production Manager NICOLE LAPALME Controller
WWW.IMAGECOMICS.COM

FOLLOW IT DOWN

SEAN KELLEY McKEEVER
CREATOR/WRITER

ALEXANDRE TEFENKGI
CREATOR/ARTIST

JEAN-FRANCOIS BEAULIEU
COLORIST

ARIANA MAHER
LETTERER

ARIELLE BASICH
EDITOR

ANDRES JUAREZ
LOGO DESIGN

CARINA TAYLOR
PRODUCTION DESIGN

OUTPOST ZERO VOLUME 2. FIRST PRINTING. May 2019. Published by Image Comics, Inc. Office of publication: 2701 NW Vaughn St., Ste. 780, Portland, OR 97210. Copyright © 2019 Skybound, LLC. Originally published in single magazine form as OUTPOST ZERO #5-9. OUTPOST ZERO™ (including all prominent characters featured herein), its logo and all character likenesses are trademarks of Skybound, LLC, unless otherwise noted. Image Comics® and its logos are registered trademarks and copyrights of Image Comics, Inc. All rights reserved. No part of this publication may be reproduced or transmitted in any form or by any means (except for short excerpts for review purposes) without the express written permission of Image Comics, Inc. All names, characters, events and locales in this publication are entirely fictional. Any resemblance to actual persons (living or dead), events or places, without satiric intent, is coincidental. Printed in the U.S.A. For information regarding the CPSIA on this printed material call: 203-595-3636. ISBN: 978-1-5343-1216-6

volume two

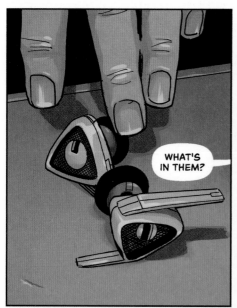

WHAT'S IN THEM?

MUSIC. *HOMEWORLD* ERA, SAYS THE METADATA. IT'S WHATEVER WAS LOADED WHEN GENSHIP OH-EIGHT *CRASH-LANDED* HERE.

NO ONE KNOWS *HOW* TO CHANGE THE LINEUP, SO *DON'T* ASK FOR--

IT'S FINE.

NOW *THESE*...

...WITH THESE YOU NEED TO BE *VERY CAREFUL.*

IT'S THE ONLY PAIR LIKE THIS WE GOT LEFT, AND WE *CANNOT* FABRICATE *NEW ONES.*

THEY AREN'T LIKE THE *INDUSTRIAL* TYPE. STAY BELOW THE *TREE LINE* OR YOU COULD BE IN REAL TROUBLE.

GOT ANY QUESTIONS?

JUST ONE.

HOW *JEALOUS* ARE YOU RIGHT NOW?

BE SAFE OUT THERE, LYSS.

WOOOOOWOO!

I was lost at sea when I saw you

I swore

I'd never seen nothing like that

like that

CAN YOU BELIEVE IT, **DEAN?** THERE'S A **CRISIS.**

THAT'S LYSS. **SERVICES TEAM** INTERN.

SERVICES? SHE DOESN'T CARE ABOUT **ANYTHING,** DOES SHE?

ALEA...

YOU GAVE ME MY PROJECTOR BACK, AND I HELD UP MY END.

I TOLD YOU HOW STEVEN WAS ABLE TO GET OUT INTO THE FROST.

IT'S OVER NOW.

I MEAN, I DON'T SEE WHAT ELSE...

I'VE BEEN TRYING TO MAKE SENSE OF IT. WHY *THIS* WAS THE LAST THING STEVEN SAID BEFORE HE STEPPED OUT OF THE AIRLOCK AND...

BEFORE HE WENT AWAY.

THERE *IS* NO MAKING SENSE OF IT.

MAYBE WE JUST DIDN'T REALLY KNOW HIM. SOME PEOPLE JUST DON'T SHOW SIGNS...

SPEAK FOR YOURSELF.

YOUR PROJECTOR, SAM. THE RECORDING OF THAT *GIRL.*

LINDA? WHAT ABOUT HER?

THE *GENSHIP ANCESTRY PROJECT--* THE *G.A.P.*

YOU SAID IT'S ALL DOWN IN THE *STEM* SOMEWHERE-- A WHOLE *LIBRARY* OF RECORDINGS FROM OUR PAST.

AND...?

DOWN IN THE STEM.

DOWN.

SO YOU THINK HE--

STEVEN DIDN'T *KNOW* I HAD THE PROJECTOR, YOU'RE THE ONLY ONE--

UNLESS *YOU* TOLD SOMEONE.

RIGHT. YOU DIDN'T FIND OUT 'TIL LATER. HE COULDN'T HAVE KNOWN.

BUT HE KNEW *SOMETHING* WE DIDN'T. HE SAID *WE* HAVE TO SAVE THEM.

US.

YOU AND ME.

IF SOMETHING MAKES EVEN A LITTLE SENSE, WE *HAVE* TO LOOK INTO IT.

I WAS RIGHT. SHOULD *NEVER* HAVE TOLD YOU WHAT HE SAID.

WHAT?

EVEN IF HE KNEW ABOUT THE *G.A.P.* SOMEHOW, AND HE KNEW *I* KNEW ABOUT IT, WHICH IS *INSANE*--

--THE CONNECTION WAS DELIBERATELY *SEVERED.* I MEANT WHAT I SAID--*NO ONE* WANTS THIS STUFF RECOVERED.

SO YOU'VE *SEEN* THIS SUPPOSED ACT OF SABOTAGE.

I FOUND THE RELAY MY PROJECTOR CONNECTS WITH, YEAH.

SO... WHERE'S THIS RELAY?

HEY!

ALEA-- IF I'M RIGHT ABOUT THIS--

WE DON'T KNOW *WHO* CUT THE CONNECTION OR WHY OR HOW MANY ARE *INVOLVED*--

WE DON'T EVEN KNOW IF THE G.A.P. IS IN ANY WAY *FUNCTIONAL.* WE'D BE IN DEEP TROUBLE OVER NOTHING.

HEY. PLEASE.

YOU'RE RIGHT. WE DON'T KNOW. BUT, SAM...

...WOULDN'T YOU *LIKE* TO KNOW?

SAM?

IT'S...

IT'S IN ONE OF THE SERVICE BUNKERS.

LOCKED.

I DON'T HAVE ACCESS ANYMORE.

THAT'S OKAY.

island of you

island of **AAA!**

YOU ALMOST *HIT* ME!

SERVICES TEAM'S BEEN CALLED IN.

GERALD-- IT'S MY DAY OFF!

NO EXCEPTIONS-- CRIMINALS, INTERNS, EVERYONE.

WE REST TODAY, WE DIE.

ALL THAT *ICE* IS STRESSING THE DOME, SO WE'RE SETTING OFF THE STEAM BANKS.

WHAT'S THAT GONNA DO?

THE HEAT'LL MAKE A LIQUID BARRIER, THEY SAY.

DISTRIBUTE THE WEIGHT, EASE THE BURDEN.

HIT THE BUNKERS. YOU GOT THIRTY-SIX TO FORTY-ONE.

AND *DON'T RUSH IT.*

DO THAT, THE STEAM BANKS'LL *BLOW.*

NNH. COME *ON...*

STUBBORN...

CRRR

THERE WE--

NOTHING.

NOTHING BACK THERE.

CRRR

HURRY, HURRY.

NO NO NO! SLOW DOWN, SLOW *DOWN.*

CRRR

HA! YOU DIDN'T GET ME, STEAM RELEASE BUNKER!

CLIC

it filled my heart with fear

all your threats and torments made it very clear

there would be no one passing through

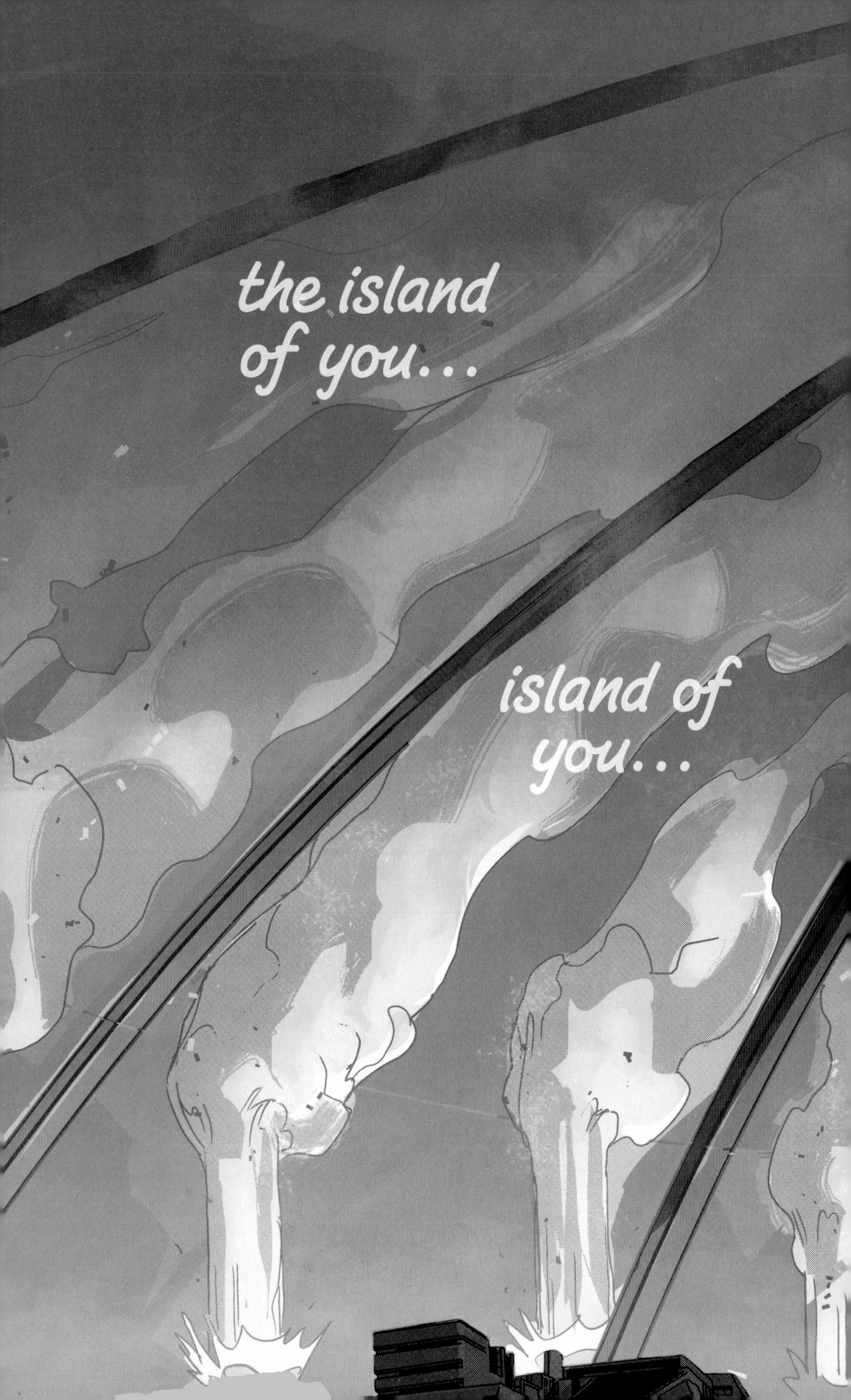
the island
of you...
island of
you...

I HAVE TO GO BACK, STRETCH MY LEGS, GET *OUT*...

JUST A FEW MORE HOURS, *JOSH*, WE NEED YOU.

I CAN'T.

I CAN'T.

YOU'RE OKAY, JUST BREATHE.

WHEN I WAS DOWN THERE? UNDER THE OUTPOST? IT WAS WEIRD.

I FELT THERE WAS, LIKE, *SOMEONE ELSE.*

BUT THERE WASN'T.

IT'S CREEPY IN GENERAL DOWN IN THOSE THINGS.

EVERYTHING ECHOES, THE COLD CUTS THROUGH YOUR CLOTHES...

YEAH. AND I WAS WEARING *THIS.*

SO, LYSS...

SAM AND I... WE'RE DOING AN EXPERIMENT. I FIGURED YOU'D BE COOL WITH GETTING US ACCESS TO THE COMMUNICATIONS RELAY BUNKER--

NO.

THAT'S IT? JUST "NO"?

I'M NOT MY BEST SELF LATELY, AND IT--

I'M TRYING, ALEA.

WITH ALL THE STUFF GOING ON, I'M TRYING, BUT I FEEL LIKE AT ANY SECOND I'M GONNA--

DENIS!

crashed hard upon your beach and

I knew

that you were going to strike me

to spike me

I braced myself to be snuffed out

when you

swore there could be nothing like me

like me

--TOO HIGH, MOMMY. IT'S TOO HIGH!

...LET IT FREE YOU.

the hazards you had made

they only served to keep yourself afraid

KRIZZ

so that no one ever knew

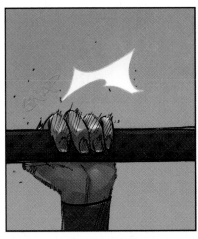

the island of you...

ARE YOU THERE, MITCHELL? AT THE END?

YOU DON'T HAVE MUCH TIME LEFT.

EVERYTHING THAT'S LED UP TO NOW IS FOR NOTHING IF YOUR HEAD JAMS UP ON YOU.

YOU **CAN'T** LET OTHER STUFF IN.

TO WIN, YOU HAVE TO **SEE** THE END.

DO YOU SEE IT?

OF COURSE.

REMEMBER, YOU CAN'T BE *HERE* TO SEE IT. YOU CAN'T BE ANYWHERE BUT *THERE*.

THERE, IN THE MOMENT, FULL CLARITY, YOUR OPPONENT LYING BEFORE YOU.

FORGET YOUR PROBLEMS.

SURVIVAL DEMANDS YOU PUT YOUR LIFE ASIDE AND--

ZWiiiiSH

I TOLD YOU...

I SEE IT.

NO, ALEA, NO WAY.

OUR DEAL WAS--

FORGET THE DEAL, THIS ISN'T--

THIS IS *POST-DEAL*, SAM.

LYSS IS MY CLOSEST FRIEND. I TRUST HER COMPLETELY.

EVERY PERSON WE TELL ABOUT THE *GENSHIP ANCESTRY PROJECT* INCREASES THE CHANCE OF THE *WRONG* PEOPLE KNOWING WE KNOW.

AND THE MORE PEOPLE KNOW I WAS THE LAST TO SEE STEVEN AND...

AND IF THEY KNOW I WAS IN THE AIRLOCK...

I'M LATE! I KNOW. SORRY.

MY PARENTS *INSIST* ON EXCAVATION WATCH BEFORE BED--TO "KEEP US APPRECIATIVE"-- SO I COULDN'T SNEAK OUT.

OKAY! SO, ARE WE READY FOR ADVENTURE AND EXCITEMENT?

THIS... DOES NOT EXCITE.

HOW ARE YOU EVEN SUPPOSED TO KNOW WHAT ANYTHING'S *FOR?*

HARD TO BELIEVE ALL OF THIS WAS *USED* ONCE. WE'RE PROBABLY GETTING BY WITH HARDLY ANY OF IT.

NO WAY TO REALLY TELL.

WHAT ARE YOU *AFTER* DOWN HERE?

ANYTHING THAT LOOKS LIKE IT MIGHT LEAD INTO THE STEM.

WE JUST KIND OF WANNA SEE WHAT'S DOWN THERE--IF WE CAN.

WE'RE ALMOST BETTER OFF *NOT* KNOWING, THOUGH, RIGHT?

SOME THINGS JUST GET ADDED TO THE LIST OF THINGS WE CAN'T DO ANYTHING ABOUT.

I MEAN, WE CAN'T EVEN CHANGE THE MUSIC ON THOSE LITTLE *EAR PLAYERS,* SO *THIS--*

UH, LYSS, *YOU* TOLD ME WE CAN'T IGNORE THE UNKNOWN BECAUSE IT'S EVERYWHERE. AND ANYWAY--

--WE'RE DOING IT BECAUSE *STEVEN* ASKED US TO.

DID YOU JUST--

I DID, IT'S DONE.

STEVEN? I... DON'T UNDER-STAND...

HE THOUGHT SAM AND I COULD FIND SOMETHING DOWN IN THE STEM TO HELP THE OUTPOST. HE SAID SO BEFORE HE...

WE'RE NOT SURE WHAT OR WHY OR HOW, BUT HE *WANTED* US TO TRY.

WHY DIDN'T YOU JUST TELL ME STEVEN WAS BEHIND THIS?

OF COURSE I'M GONNA HELP...

YOU'RE RIGHT. WE *SHOULD* HAVE SAID SO FROM THE START. BUT SAM DOESN'T REALLY KNOW US YET.

HEY, THAT'S... YOU KNOW, YOU *ARE* GONNA FIND OUT YOU CAN TRUST US. SERIOUS.

THIS IS A GOOD THING, SAM. TAKE IT.

THIS USED TO TALK TO AN INFO HUB IN THE STEM. BUT, SEE, IT WAS *SABOTAGED.* IT'S USELESS NOW.

HOW DO YOU KNOW ALL--

YOU CAN'T TELL *ANYBODY,* LYSS. EVERYTHING I'M TELLING YOU, SHOWING YOU?

NOT YOUR *FAMILY,* YOUR *FRIENDS*--

TAKE IT EASY, SAM. SHE *UNDERSTANDS.*

LET'S TRY TAKING OFF THE BASE COVER.

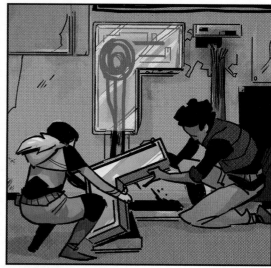

WE'D HAVE TO TAKE THE WHOLE THING APART.

WHICH COULD BREAK SOMETHING IMPORTANT.

MIGHT, YEAH.

JUST WONDERING... DOES IT MATTER WHERE YOU GET TO THE STEM *FROM?*

TWO MORE DEGREES AND--

NO POWER?!

DID WE LOSE THEM?

KIDS! WHERE ARE YOU?!

NOT AGAIN!

EVERYTHING'S ALRIGHT! IT'S JUST ANOTHER BROWNOUT!

POWER WILL RETURN SHORTLY!

HEY. HEY, ARE YOU--?

WHAT?

IT'S YOU. YOUR *DEBUT'S* COMING UP.

YEAH. I'M AWARE.

THERE HASN'T BEEN A FIGHT SINCE THE CELL.

EVERYONE'S SO--WELL, YOU KNOW.

JUST WANTED TO SAY THANK YOU. WE NEED IT.

KNOW HOW MANY FIGHTERS LIVE TO SEE THEIR TWENTIETH BIRTHDAY, MITCHELL?

OR *KNOW* IT'S THEIR TWENTIETH?

YOU'RE ONE OF THE COMPLAINERS ALL OF A SUDDEN?

WHAT, BECAUSE *I'M* FIGHTING?

I'LL BE SO GOOD I'LL NEVER GET HIT ONCE. YOU'LL SEE.

I DON'T PLAN TO SIT THERE AND SEE YOU--

JUST BECAUSE YOU THINK THIS IS WHAT YOU *WANT* FROM LIFE--

NO, YOU'RE RIGHT.

WHAT I *REALLY* WANT DEEP DOWN IS *FARMING TEAM.*

AFTER ALL, IT'S BEEN SUCH A *BOON* TO OUR FAMILY.

AND LOOK AT WHAT AN EXCITING GUY IT MADE *YOU.*

THIS SOME KIND OF **PRANK?!**

HEY.

FIRST STEVEN, NOW YOU'RE GONNA INFECT MY **FRIENDS?** IS **THAT** WHAT YOU'RE DOING, **SAM?**

HEY.

WHAT'S **WRONG** WITH YOU?

ME?!

YOU'RE SPENDING TIME WITH THAT WEAK, LITTLE--

DID YOU NOT **SEE** HIM AFTER HIS PARENTS DIED?

MOST PATHETIC, SPINELESS THING **EVER!** HE'S GONNA **BRING YOU DOWN!**

WHAT? OH, I'M WRONG? **TELL** ME I'M WRONG!

MITCHELL...

YOUR TIRELESS EFFORTS WITH THE SPECIAL JOINT EMERGENCY TEAM HAVE BEEN APPRECIATED BY ALL.

THANK YOU FOR YOUR SERVICE TO THE OUTPOST, JOSH. WE'RE LUCKY TO HAVE YOU.

THEY *NEED* THIS MORE THAN EVER.

A FRESH FACE, A FRESH WIN.

HOW ARE YOU GONNA DO IT?

SEE IT.

SEE WHAT?

SEE THE END.

THE MOMENT, MY OPPONENT LYING BEFORE ME.

BE THERE.

YOU GOT IT. NOW CLOSE YOUR EYES.

I WANT YOU TO TELL ME...

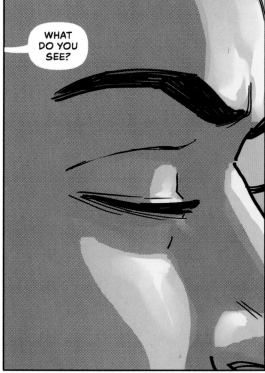

WHAT DO YOU SEE?

--HERE FOR HIS DEBUT, YOUR NEW CHALLENGER!

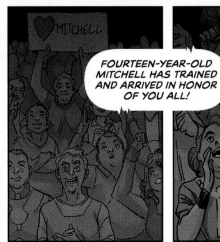

MITCHELL

FOURTEEN-YEAR-OLD MITCHELL HAS TRAINED AND ARRIVED IN HONOR OF YOU ALL!

LET HIM HEAR YOUR APPRECIATION!

NOW, THE CHALLENGER'S FIRST TEST OF WHAT WE HOPE WILL BE MANY TO COME...

...HERE'S ANTOINE!

FIFTEEN-YEAR-OLD ANTOINE HAS NOTCHED UP FIVE IMPRESSIVE WINS IN A ROW.

ASKED WHAT INSPIRES HIM TO KEEP FIGHTING, HE SAYS, "BECAUSE EVERY ONE OF US IS FIGHTING!"

NOW, WITHOUT FURTHER DELAY...

THAT SHOULD BE PLENTY.

THERE WE GO.

THE HARD PART'S FINALLY OVER.

EXPEDITION TO OUTPOST: WE'VE REACHED DAYLIGHT.

AND YOU THOUGHT IT WOULDN'T WORK...

I WAS *CONCERNED* IT WOULDN'T WORK. THERE'S A DIFFERENCE.

CHIEF, SCAN OF YOUR TABLET LOOKS GOOD, AND I LOADED THE LATEST VIDCLIP COMPILATION.

THANKS, VIVIEN. ANYTHING UNUSUAL?

FOR SAM?

UNUSUAL'S ONE WAY TO PUT IT.

I THINK HE'S FINALLY MADE SOME *FRIENDS.*

BRINGING LYSS INTO THE FOLD--BE HONEST, SAM.

STILL ANNOYED, BUT...YEAH.

GOOD MOVE.

MUST BE NICE TO HAVE YOUR PARENTS HOME.

JUST A DAY OR TWO WHILE THEY GET READY FOR WHAT'S NEXT. I'LL BARELY SEE THEM, SO WHATEVER.

I MEAN, OF COURSE--*ANY* TIME WITH THEM, I'LL TAKE IT...

SO, DID YOU GET THE WAREHOUSE CODE FROM YOUR CH--

FROM KAREN?

SHE UPDATED HER TABLET'S PASSKEY. AND ASKING NICELY WON'T WORK.

OKAY, BUT...WE *HAVE* TO GET IN, RIGHT?

THERE HAS TO BE *SOMETHING* IN THE WAREHOUSE THAT CAN GET US AROUND THE BUNKER GRATE.

HOW ELSE CAN WE SEE IF THERE'S A WAY DOWN INTO THE *STEM* IF WE DON'T--

SAM...?

HEY, ALEA.

DO YOU KNOW WHERE TO FIND SOME ROPE?

YOU'RE GOING SOMEWHERE?

WHY? IS SOMETHING...?

NO, I JUST THOUGHT WE'D--

HOW'VE YOU BEEN?

I DUNNO. FINE.

I CAME UP WITH THIS IDEA-- LIKE, FOR A CLASS PROJECT. IT'S GONNA BE SO--

ANYWAY...

IS EVERYTHING OKAY? LIKE, WITH YOU?

YEAH. NO, IT'S--

YEAH. YEAH.

YOU GO AHEAD.

I'LL BE HOME FOR DINNER!

HAVE FUN.

HEY! LYSS!

WHERE'RE YOU HEADING OFF TO?

MITCHELL.

HI.

YOU LOOK--

MY MOM'S REALLY GOOD AT HER JOB. IT'S LIKE YOU WERE BARELY IN A FIGHT.

SHE SAID YOU WERE REALLY SOMETHING...

I DIDN'T EXPECT YOU THERE, CONSIDERING. THANKS FOR ACKNOWLEDGING MY EXISTENCE, AT LEAST, UNLIKE ALEA.

I PROMISE I WON'T GET ALL--

I JUST-- I NEED YOU TO TELL ME ONE LITTLE THING...

WHAT'S GOING ON? WHAT ARE YOU GUYS UP TO WITH HIM? AM I NOT EVEN ALLOWED TO KNOW?

MITCHELL...

IT'S NOT FOR ME TO TELL.

YOU DO LOOK GOOD, I MEAN IT.

PLEASE DON'T. YOU KNOW HOW SAM CAN BE...

HE'S SAD-- DON'T WANT TO MAKE HIM WORSE. NOW HE'S HAPPY-- WOULDN'T WANT TO RUIN THAT.

HE CAN'T BE DISTRACTED RIGHT NOW. HE'S INSULAR. HE'S DIFFICULT.

PART OF BEING A DOCTOR IS THAT I'LL TAKE A WHOLE LOT OF SECRETS WHEN I GO.

BUT WHAT YOU HAVE TO SAY TO SAM, THAT WON'T LEAVE WITH ME. OTHERS KNOW IT, TOO.

EACH NEW DAY BRINGS A CHANCE THAT SOMEONE ELSE WILL SAY SOMETHING TO HIM.

I CAN ONLY IMAGINE THE HUMILIATION YOUR SWEET BOY WOULD SUFFER, KNOWING YOU COULD HAVE TOLD HIM ALL THIS TIME BUT WOULDN'T.

THAT'S NOT FAIR. YOU DON'T KNOW.

OH, SURE I KNOW.

IT'S AN AWKWARD SUBJECT, AND YOU CAN RATIONALIZE THAT AN OMISSION ISN'T *TECHNICALLY* LYING.

BUT IF YOU WERE TO BROACH THE SUBJECT, SAM WILL HAVE QUESTIONS...

...AND THEN YOU'D HAVE TO DECIDE WHETHER YOU'RE GOING TO LIE TO HIM *OUTRIGHT.*

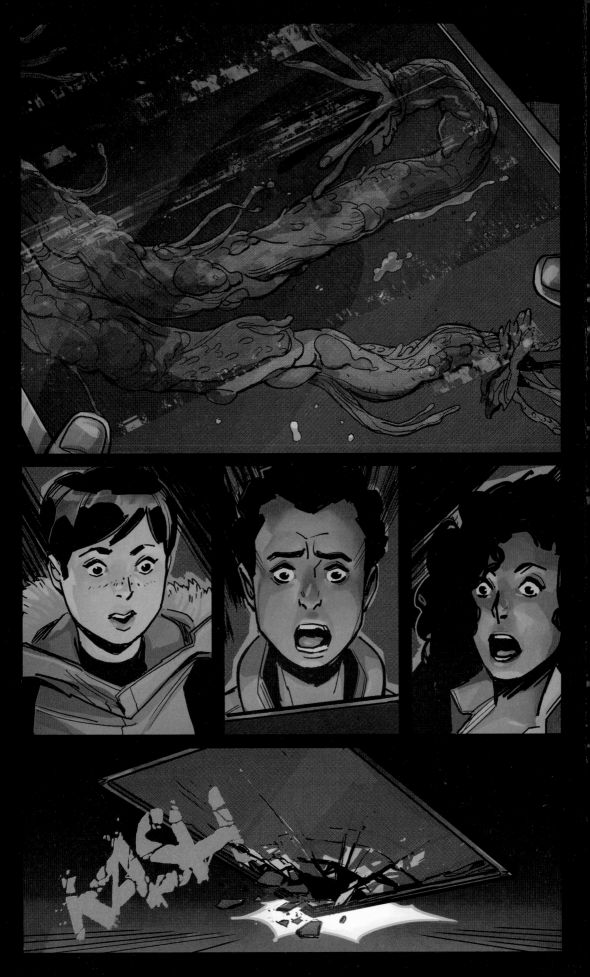

EXPLAIN HOW IT WAS *BEFORE* SAM'S MOTHER. THAT HE WAS FAITHFUL.

IT'LL BE DIFFICULT AT FIRST, BUT HE *WILL* APPRECIATE IT. HE'LL COME TO SEE YOU IN A DIFFERENT LIGHT.

AND WHEN HE ASKS *WHY* WE DIDN'T STAY TOGETHER? I'M SUPPOSED TO TELL HIM WHAT?

YOU COULD SAY IT DOESN'T MATTER. THAT YOUR BREAK-UP MADE HIS EXISTENCE POSSIBLE.

YOU COULD TELL HIM WHAT YOU TOLD *HIS FATHER*--THAT YOU WERE *INFERTILE,* THAT HE NEEDED TO FIND SOMEONE TO REPRODUCE WITH.

OR I COULD TELL HIM I WAS SELFISH AND AFRAID. THAT I PUT MYSELF BEFORE OUR SPECIES' SURVIVAL.

THAT I MADE YOU COMPLICIT IN A LIE--NOT JUST TO HIS FATHER, BUT TO THE ENTIRE OUTPOST.

BECAUSE I DIDN'T *WANT* A CHILD.

THAT PART IS A SECRET THAT *CAN* LEAVE WITH ME.

IF YOU'D LIKE IT TO.

FORGET WHAT I SAID ABOUT THE SKY.

I COULD NEVER TIRE OF OUR OWN SUNSETS.

THE CALIBRATIONS ARE OFF! I *TOLD* FABRICATION TEAM TO--

STOP ALREADY, KAANAN.

YOU CAN COVER YOUR ASS LATER.

THERE. IT'S OFF.

TAP

I'M *NOT* COVERING MY-- I'M *ANALYZING* THE *SITUATION.*

WE'RE GOING TO NEED TO FIX THE--

POC

DAMN IT--

IT TOOK FIVE DAYS, BUT THEY EVENTUALLY VAPORIZED THE WATER AND GOT BACK IN THROUGH THE AIRLOCK.

CAN'T STOP THINKING ABOUT WHAT IT WOULD HAVE BEEN LIKE, BEING ONE OF THEM.

BEING KAANAN.

THERE'S A DIFFERENCE, ISN'T THERE?

THE ABSTRACT IDEA OF DYING IN THE FROST, VERSUS CONFRONTING THE REALITY OF IT.

YOU KNOW WHAT THAT'S LIKE. I DO, A LITTLE.

KAANAN DROWNED IN ICE WATER, AND I THOUGHT, "GLAD IT WASN'T ME".

SAME AS AFTER WATCHING YOU WALK OUT THERE.

THING IS, STEVEN...

TURNS OUT I DON'T WANT TO DIE.

BUT WHY DO I STILL *FEEL* LIKE I DO?

FEEL LIKE WHAT?

SORRY. THAT'S NOSY. I'M BEING NOSY.

YOU'RE UP LATE.

I HAVEN'T SLEPT MUCH LATELY, AFTER WHAT WE SAW.

WE DON'T KNOW WHAT WE SAW.

IT WAS *ALIVE*, SAM. IT WAS... AWFUL.

HAVE YOU SAID ANYTHING TO ANYONE?

YOU AND ALEA SAID NOT TO. SO, NO.

THEY PUT STEVEN'S PORTRAIT AWAY.

IT'S KAANAN'S TURN TO BE MOURNED NOW. THERE'S USUALLY LESS TIME ON DISPLAY THAN HE HAD BECAUSE OF--

COPYCATS. YEAH.

I SHOULD SLEEP.

SAM?

I TOLD ALEA, NOW I'M TELLING YOU...

DON'T GO DOWN THERE. WHATEVER THAT IS BENEATH US...

...IT'S DEATH.

I'VE BEEN SLOWLY GOING *INSANE.*

MY PARENTS WERE OUT THERE AND I COULDN'T *DO* ANYTHING-- COULDN'T *HELP.*

AND WHAT WE SAW-- CAN'T DO ANYTHING ABOUT *THAT* CAUSE MY HEAD'S NOT ON STRAIGHT AND PEOPLE ARE CHECKING ON ME AND ELLA NIGHT AND DAY...

AND WHERE'VE *YOU* BEEN? HIDING FROM ME? I WANNA FIND MORE WIRE SPOOLS. TAKE ANOTHER *LOOK.*

Y'KNOW, ALEA...I DON'T...

WHAT, ARE YOU *LYSS* NOW? ARE YOU FREAKED OUT?

WE DISCOVERED LIFE, SAM. *LIFE.*

YOU DON'T *KNOW* THAT.

ONLY BECAUSE *YOU* BROKE--

ONLY BECAUSE YOU BROKE THE TABLET AND WE LOST THE RECORDING.

BUT IF WE REPEAT THE EXPERIMENT, WE CAN CONFIRM. IT'S SIMPLE.

I DON'T KNOW. KAREN'S CLAMPING DOWN ON ME FOR SOME REASON.

SHE'S EVEN CHECKED OUT MY ROOM.

THE PROJECTOR?

I MADE A BETTER HIDING SPOT. AFTER IT WAS *STOLEN* FROM ME.

PLEASE, SAM. WE'LL BE MORE CAUTIOUS, TAKE OUR TIME...

EVEN IF YOU DON'T BUY WHAT STEVEN SAID, YOU'RE *CURIOUS.*

WELL, IT'S NOT THAT I--

I MEAN, I DUNNO. MAYBE...

MAYBE WE SHOULD JUST GET BACK TO OUR LIVES.

YOU KNOW, KAANAN THOUGHT HE ALMOST HAD THESE POWER FLUCTUATIONS FIGURED OUT.

I DON'T SUPPOSE ANYONE ELSE IN PLANNING TEAM HAS THE BRAIN TO TACKLE HIS DATA.

NOT TO SPEAK ILL, BUT HE WAS KIND OF OFF-BASE.

DID HE TELL YOU HIS THEORY?

HE SAID THE ICE STORM AND BROWNOUTS WERE A TOTAL COINCIDENCE.

THAT THE DATA SUPPORTED AN ELECTROMAGNETIC ANOMALY THAT'S BEEN GROWING FOR YEARS...

HEY, LIGHT'S ON.

WHERE ARE YOU GOING?

NEED TO CHECK ON SOMETHING.

THE POWER WASN'T REALLY HER FAULT, DAD.

OH, ELLA. A PERFECTLY RANDOM OPPORTUNITY TO BLAME SOMETHING ON YOUR SISTER AND YOU TURN IT DOWN?

I DON'T EVEN KNOW YOU ANYMORE.

YOU'RE NEVER FUNNY.

...I DON'T KNOW HOW OR WHY, BUT THIS IS WHAT I AM NOW.

I CAN'T GO BACK.

...I DON'T KNOW HOW OR WHY, BUT THIS IS WHAT I AM NOW.

ARE YOU AWAKE?

I KNOW I'VE BEEN... WORSE LATELY. QUIET.

WHATEVER IT IS, YOU CAN TELL ME.

SOMETIMES I WISH...I COULD FIND THE REST OF US. GO TO OTHER WORLDS.

WHEN I THINK ABOUT HOW I DON'T GET TO EXPERIENCE ANY OF IT. THAT I'M... *HERE*...

IT HURTS.

YOU'VE ALWAYS BEEN INQUISITIVE. YOU *SEE* MORE THAN MOST PEOPLE.

ALL THAT IS WHAT GOT ME WANDERING FROM MY FAMILY WHEN THE CELL CAME.

YOU COULDN'T HAVE SAVED THEM.

YEAH, BUT SOMETIMES I THINK MAYBE I WAS...

I JUST WANT...

WHY CAN'T I JUST BE NORMAL?

SAM...

DON'T YOU EVER BE THAT.

DON'T YOU DARE.

I HEAR WHAT YOU'RE TELLING ME...

...AND IT ALL SOUNDS LOGICAL AND VERY SCIENTIFIC, BUT I HAVE A DUTY TO REMIND YOU THAT SCIENCE IS HARDLY AN *EXACT* SCIENCE FOR US.

THAT'S NOT ENTIRELY FAIR--

NO?

DIDN'T WE JUST PROVE OUT THERE THAT, WHEN IT COMES TO UNDERSTANDING OUR ANCESTORS' TECH, WE'RE A BUNCH OF NOVICES?

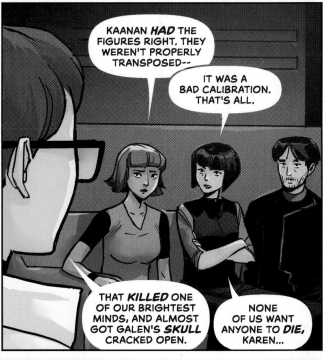

KAANAN *HAD* THE FIGURES RIGHT. THEY WEREN'T PROPERLY TRANSPOSED--

IT WAS A BAD CALIBRATION. THAT'S ALL.

THAT *KILLED* ONE OF OUR BRIGHTEST MINDS, AND ALMOST GOT GALEN'S *SKULL* CRACKED OPEN.

NONE OF US WANT ANYONE TO *DIE*, KAREN...

...BUT WE CAN'T SIT HERE AND LET *ALL* OF US DIE BECAUSE WE'RE AFRAID TO RISK A FEW VOLUNTEERS WHO WANT TO DO SOMETHING ABOUT IT.

OKAY, KAANAN... LET'S LOOK AT THOSE DATA CHARTS OF YOURS AGAIN.

I FEEL LIKE I NEED TO KEEP REPEATING MYSELF TO YOU...

MY JOB IS TO *SECURE* THE OUTPOST. EVERY TIME WE OPEN THAT AIRLOCK, WE PLACE *EVERYONE* IN DANGER.

IT'S AN *AIRLOCK*, KAREN. IT'S *DESIGNED* TO BE *SAFE*.

DESIGNED BY EXPERTS *WE* CAN'T CONSULT WITH TO ENSURE IT *REMAINS* SAFE.

I'M SAYING WE HAVE TO BE *CAUTIOUS*.

I THANK YOU FOR WHAT YOU'RE ALL DOING, REALLY, I DO...

...BUT WE'RE GOING OVER THE PLAN AGAIN AND AGAIN UNTIL I'M *SURE* YOUR NEXT TRIP OUTSIDE ACTUALLY *FIXES* THINGS.

ANOTHER THING--SALVAGE MORE CAMS. WE NEED FEWER BLIND SPOTS.

WHY? WE GOT A PROBLEM?

ASSUME WE'VE *ALWAYS* GOT A PROBLEM.

I COULD STAND HERE ALL NIGHT, EVERY NIGHT.

BUT YOU'RE SAYING YOU *JUMPED* FROM HERE, AND SURVIVED BECAUSE OF THE GRAVSYNC.

EXCEPT YOU GOT HURT BECAUSE YOUR *CALCULATIONS* WERE OFF, BECAUSE OF AN *ANOMALY* THAT'S CAUSING THE BROWNOUTS.

PRETTY MUCH. AND HERE'S THE LAST BIT.

I KNOW *WHERE* THE ANOMALY IS.

INSIDE THE SCRAP WAREHOUSE.

BUT I NEVER SAW... WHAT COULD IT *BE?*

YOU WANNA KNOW. YOU *HAVE* TO KNOW.

I DON'T HAVE ACCESS ANYMORE.

YEAH, BUT LOOK.

HERE'S WHAT I'M THINKING, AND IT SOUNDS COMPLETELY CRAZY, BUT HEAR ME OUT...

RUN AND JUMP.

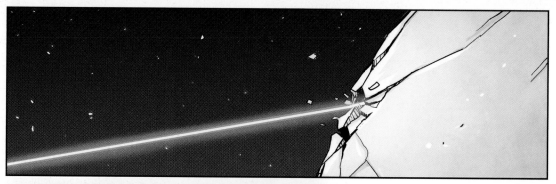

ENGINEERING TEAM SAYS THERE'S ALREADY A SIGNIFICANT REDUCTION IN DOME PRESSURE.

IT'S NOT OVER, BUT AS LONG AS WE'RE MONITORING, THERE SHOULDN'T BE SURPRISES.

THANK YOU.

IF THAT'S ALL, CHIEF, THEN WE'LL START PLOTTING OUR NEXT EXCURSION, THERE'S REASON TO BELIEVE OUR *LAST* TRIP MIGHT HAVE--

DENIS.

JANN.

THIS CELL DIDN'T HURT US AS BADLY AS THE LAST, BUT IT WAS ALMOST THE *END* OF US.

OUR PRIORITY *NOW* IS MAKING US SAFER WHEN THE *NEXT* CELL HITS. AND WITH *KAANAN* GONE...

WE'RE STILL ON *PLANNING TEAM* DUTY, YOU MEAN. WAS THIS A *COUNCIL* DECISION?

IT'S NOT THE *ONLY* DECISION THE COUNCIL MADE.

I'M SORRY, ALEA.

IT WAS INEVITABLE, RIGHT? *EVERYONE* QUESTIONED THE NEED FOR DISCOVERY TEAM. EVEN YOU, MITCHELL, STEVEN...

NOW IT DOESN'T *HAVE* TO BE QUESTIONED ANYMORE, I GUESS.

DISCOVERY TEAM IS GONE.

DOES THAT MEAN...? ARE *YOU* DONE, TOO? EXPLORING WITH SAM?

THE STUFF WE'RE DOING, IT'S... A PASTIME, LYSS.

CURIOSITY.

NO ONE'S GETTING HURT.

SO YOU'RE SAYING THAT *THING* WE SAW ISN'T *DANGEROUS?* OR ARE YOU LIKE *SAM* NOW, DENYING WE EVEN SAW *ANYTHING?*

THAT'S NOT WHAT HE'S--

SAM'S... CAREFUL. THAT'S ALL.

I *CAN'T* IGNORE WHAT'S OUT THERE.

I PROMISE, WHATEVER WE DO, WE'LL BE SAFE.

BUT I *HAVE* TO KEEP LOOKING. I HAVE TO.

YOU CAN *JOIN* US AGAIN IF YOU CHANGE YOUR MIND.

I WON'T SAY IT WASN'T FUN FOR A WHILE...

HAVE YOU SPOKEN TO MITCHELL?

NOT SINCE BEFORE HIS FIGHT, HARDLY KNOW WHERE I'D EVEN FIND HIM ANYMORE, CERTAINLY NOT HERE.

PRETTY SOON *WE* WON'T BE HERE ANYMORE, EITHER, FULL-TIME INTERNS...

YEAH...

HONESTLY, IF IT WASN'T FOR BEING FRIENDS WITH HIS SISTER, IF IT WASN'T FOR STEVEN...

WOULD SOMEONE LIKE MITCHELL EVEN *BE* MY FRIEND?

BUT HE IS YOUR FRIEND.

I KNOW HE *SHOWS* IT IN WEIRD WAYS, BUT SO DO I SOMETIMES.

YOU'VE GOT A POINT, I'M STUCK WITH BOTH OF YOU, AREN'T I?

PEOPLE KEEP SAYING THINGS ARE GONNA GET BACK TO NORMAL NOW.

THAT'D BE NICE, WOULDN'T IT? IT'LL NEVER BE THE WAY IT WAS, BUT IT COULD BE CLOSE.

ANYWAY...

I HOPE THEY'RE RIGHT.

I'VE...BEEN TRYING TO HACK YOUR PERSONAL TABLET. I WANTED ACCESS TO THE WAREHOUSE, SO I COULD MAKE STUFF.

I'M SORRY.

SO THERE'S THAT. *AND* THE AIRLOCK.

SEEMS TO BE A *PATTERN* WITH YOU.

I WANT TO TRUST YOU, SAM. SECURITY TEAM IS TOO IMPORTANT FOR THAT TRUST TO BE UNCONDITIONAL.

BUT YOU CONFESSED *PROACTIVELY* TO ONE OF YOUR WRONGS.

AND THAT'S SOMETHING, SO...

PROVISIONAL INTERNSHIP. WELCOME BACK.

BUT IF YOU WERE ANYBODY ELSE, YOU'D BE OUT, UNDERSTAND ME? *NO MORE TROUBLE.*

YES, CHIEF. THANK YOU.

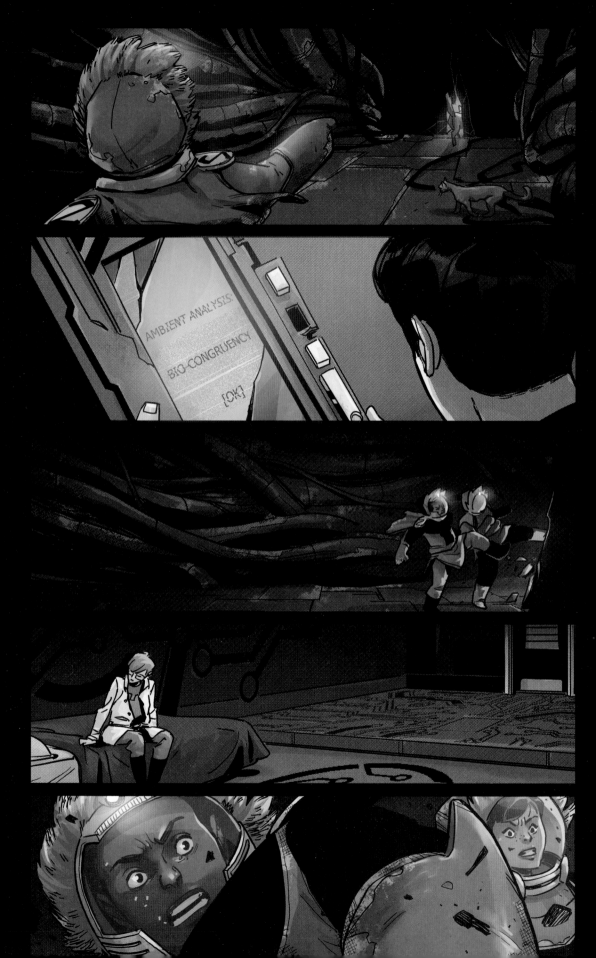

AMBIENT ANALYSIS.

BIO-CONGRUENCY

[OK]

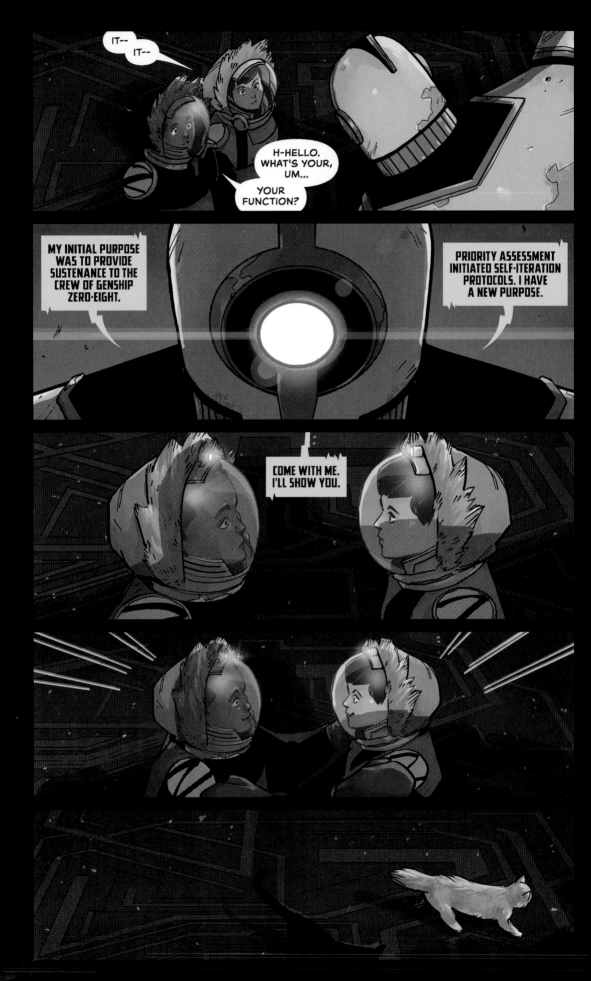

to be
continued

we bury us,
we bury
everyone.

GENSHIP

MAX POP. 1 MILLION

BIOME

A. DOWNTOWN
B. INDUSTRIAL QUADRANT
C. FARMING QUADRANT
D. HOUSING QUAD. ALPHA
E. HOUSING QUAD. BETA
F. LIGHT VEHICLE AIRLOCK

STEM COUPLING

G. GRAV-SYNC ENGINES
H. CREW QUARTERS
I. DOCKING PORT

B

BIOME

SURFACE
LEVEL

C

STEM
COUPLING

F

THE
OUTPOST
POP. ~10K

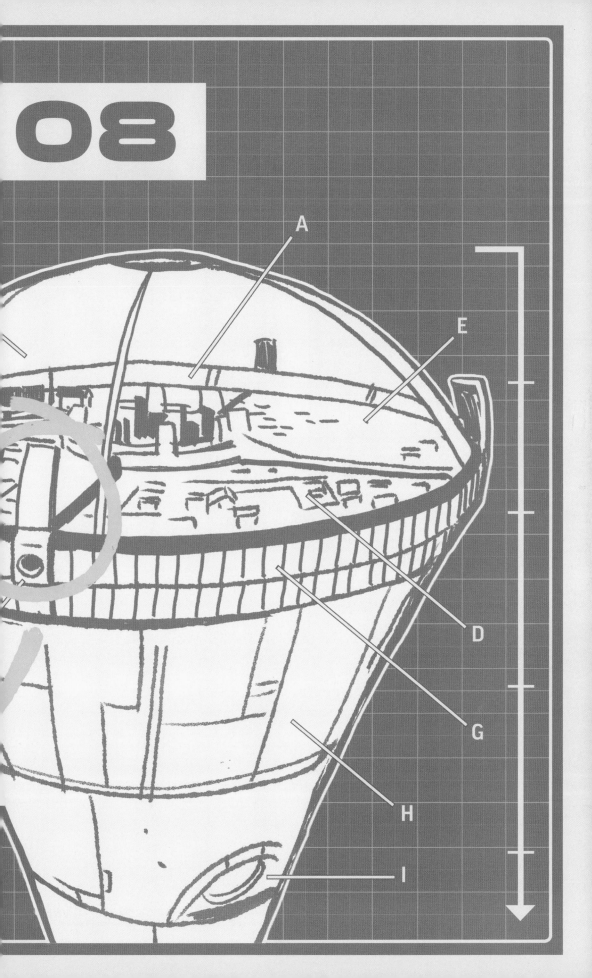

For more tales from ROBERT KIRKMAN and SKYBOUND

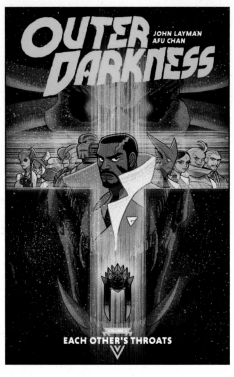

VOL. 1: EACH OTHER'S THROATS
ISBN: 978-1-5343-1210-4
$16.99

CHAPTER ONE
ISBN: 978-1-5343-0642-4
$9.99

CHAPTER TWO
ISBN: 978-1-5343-1057-5
$16.99

VOL. 1: HOMECOMING TP
ISBN: 978-1-63215-231-2
$9.99

VOL. 2: CALL TO ADVENTURE TP
ISBN: 978-1-63215-446-0
$12.99

VOL. 3: ALLIES AND ENEMIES TP
ISBN: 978-1-63215-683-9
$12.99

VOL. 4: FAMILY HISTORY TP
ISBN: 978-1-63215-871-0
$12.99

VOL. 5: BELLY OF THE BEAST TP
ISBN: 978-1-5343-0218-1
$12.99

VOL. 6: FATHERHOOD TP
ISBN: 978-1-53430-498-7
$14.99

VOL. 7: BLOOD BROTHERS TP
ISBN: 978-1-5343-1053-7
$14.99

VOL. 1: DEEP IN THE HEART TP
ISBN: 978-1-5343-0331-7
$16.99

VOL. 2: THE EYES UPON YOU TP
ISBN: 978-1-5343-0665-3
$16.99

VOL. 3: LONGHORNS TP
ISBN: 978-1-5343-1050-6
$16.99

VOL. 1: ARTIST TP
ISBN: 978-1-5343-0242-6
$16.99

VOL. 2: WARRIOR TP
ISBN: 978-1-5343-0506-9
$16.99

VOL. 1
ISBN: 978-1-60706-420-6
$9.99

VOL. 2
ISBN: 978-1-60706-568-5
$14.99

VOL. 3
ISBN: 978-1-60706-667-5
$12.99

VOL. 4
ISBN: 978-1-60706-843-3
$12.99